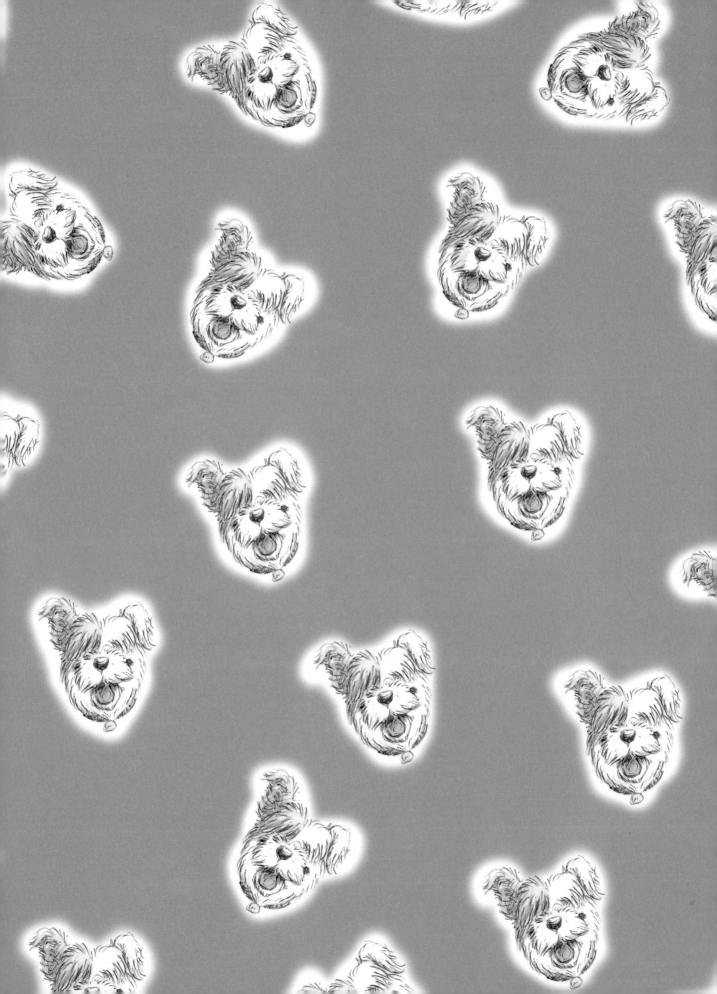

Wisteria Jane
BINGO DID IT!

Written by
AMBER HARRIS

Illustrated by
ARD HOYT

Redleaf Lane

To Timothy Baker, the man who taught me to dream big. I love you, Dad.
—Amber

To my friend Greg Bench
—Ard

Published by Redleaf Lane
An imprint of Redleaf Press
10 Yorkton Court
Saint Paul, MN 55117
www.RedleafLane.org

Text © 2016 by Amber Harris
Illustration © 2016 by Ard Hoyt

First edition 2016
Book jacket and interior design by Jim Handrigan
Main body text set in ITC Bookman Std Light

Manufactured in the United States of America
23 22 21 20 19 18 17 16   1 2 3 4 5 6 7 8

Library of Congress Control Number: 2016931742

My name is Wisteria Jane Hummell.

My dog, Bingo, is the best dog in the whole world.

Sometimes we play princess, and he is my dragon.
Bingo just loves to dress up.

One day we were having a tea party with Momma's old teacups. I told Bingo to be extra careful, but he didn't listen. That dog went and knocked the whole table over.

Momma came running. "What in the world is going on?" she asked.

"Bingo did it, Momma," I said. "He was drinking his tea like a good dog, and then he knocked everything over like a bad dog."

Momma stood there just looking at me, Bingo, and the whole big old mess. "Well, Wisty Jane," Momma said, "Bingo isn't going to help sweep this up. It looks like the two of us have some work to do."

I gave Bingo a real mad look to let him know he should *not* have broken the teacups.

After lunch, Bingo and I decided to play outside.
Bingo started digging a little hole, and that got
me to thinking it sure would be fun to dig for
buried treasure.

Next thing I knew, I heard Momma say, "Wisteria Jane Hummell, did you dig up my flower bed?"

"Momma," I said, "Bingo started the hole."

Momma took a deep breath, and she blew it out real slow. She said, "Wisty, you blamed Bingo when your tea party didn't turn out. Now you're blaming Bingo for digging up the flowers. Do you really think this is all Bingo's fault?"

I told her, "Bingo ruined the tea party when he broke the teacups. *He's* the one who dug the hole first. All I did was make it a little bigger."

Momma sat down beside me and said, "Bingo may have started the hole, Wisty, but you dug up the flowers. He probably bumped the tea table while you were squeezing him into that dress.
You need to take some responsibility for what's happened, Wisty.
Do you know what 'taking responsibility' means?"

I was so glad she asked, because I surely did not.

Momma said, "Taking responsibility means seeing how your actions affect everyone else. It means owning up to your part of the mess, and not getting mad at other people when things go wrong for you."

"Like the time you didn't put your purse away and Bingo ate five whole packs of gum, but you said it wasn't really Bingo's fault?"

"Or the time I helped Daddy wash the car, but he didn't get mad when I washed the inside too?"

Momma chuckled and said I am catching on quick
when it comes to taking responsibility.

Then she told me I needed a bath.

Sitting in that big bubbly bathtub all by myself got
me to thinking it would be real helpful of me to
give Bingo a bath too.

And this is when I knew Momma would *not* be happy about my help.

I was just about to say that the soapy mess was really Bingo's fault, but then I remembered what Momma told me about taking responsibility.

So I took a deep breath, and I blew it out real slow. I said, "Momma, I should have waited for you, but I was trying to do something nice by giving Bingo his bath. He is *not* easy to work with."

Momma said she was glad I was taking responsibility for the bubble disaster, but I still had to help clean up the mess.

I bet you'll never guess what that silly dog did next . . .

He most definitely needs to learn
about taking responsibility.

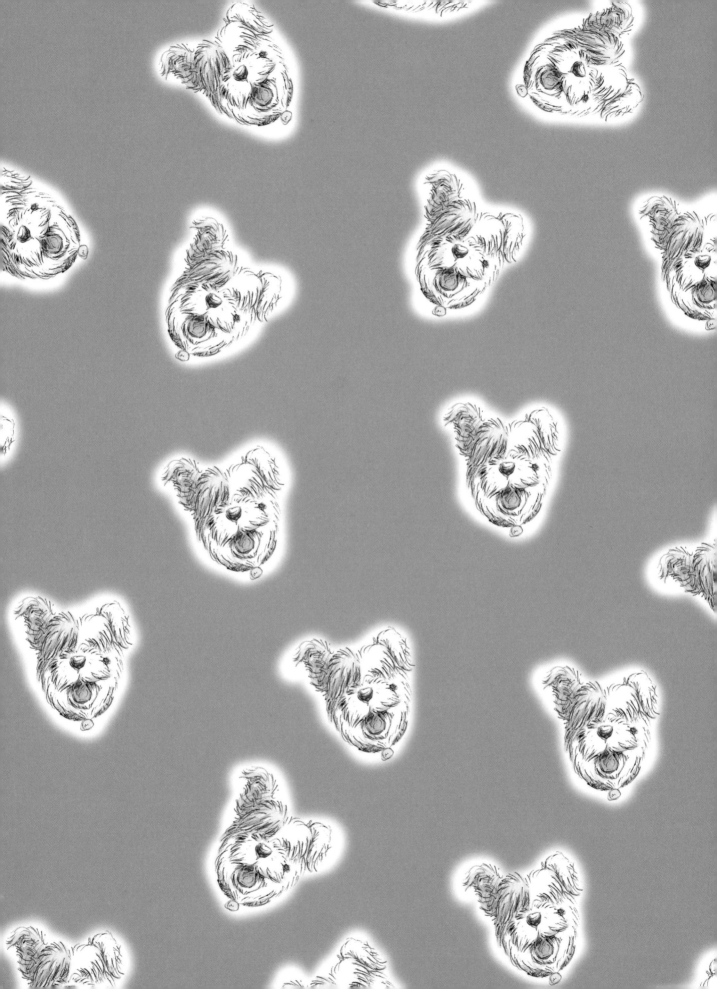

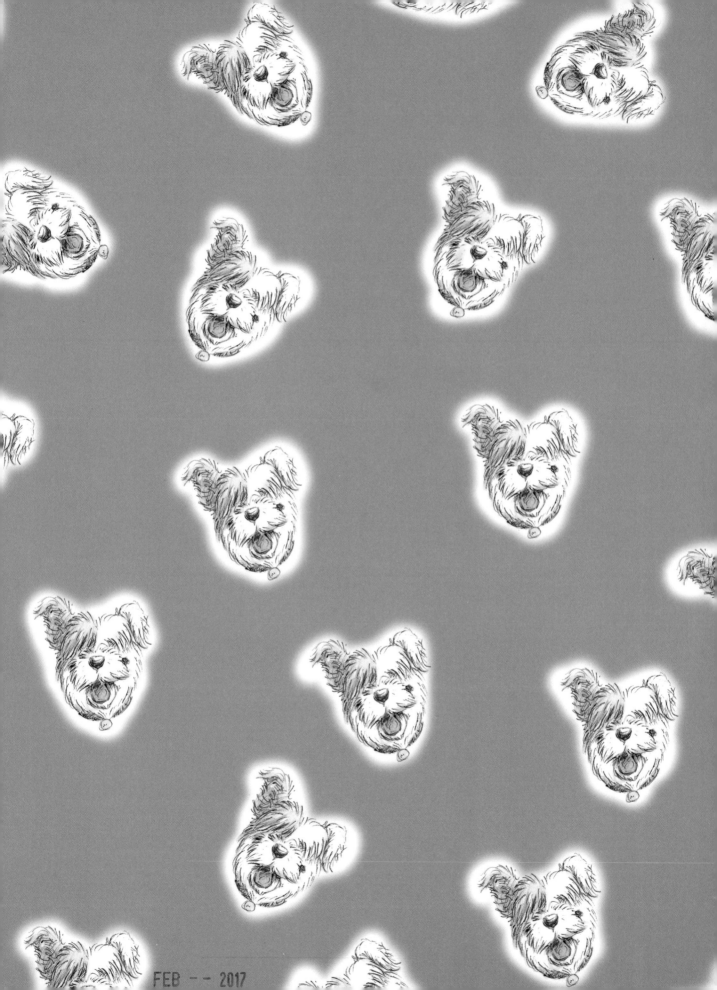

FEB – – 2017